TERRY DEARY

PIRATE TALES

THE PIRATE PRISONER

Illustrated by Helen Flook

BLOOMSBURY EDUCATION
AN IMPRINT OF BLOOMSBURY

LONDON OXFORD NEW YORK NEW DELHI SYDNEY

CHAPTER ONE
SAND AND SLAVE

Nevis Island, Caribbean, 1680

It was hot. The sun burned down on Nevis
Island and made steam rise up from the
forests. The girl ran along the yellow-grey
sands, her thin dress flapping around her
skinny legs.

"I'm going to be late," she panted. "I mustn't be late." Her dark brown skin was shining with sweat. "I have to save him. Have to. Have to."

She reached the edge of the small town and raced along the dusty streets, past the poor wooden shacks...

past the fine stone houses of the rich folk... and up to the great stone building in the centre.

A soldier stood guard at the great doors. He swatted flies that buzzed around his head. "Can I go in?" the girl begged.

"I'm not stopping you," the soldier said with a shrug.

"Has the trial started?" she asked.

The man just shrugged again. "How would I know?"

"Because you're on guard. You're here to stop people getting in," she said, crossly.

"No, I'm not. I'm here to stop the wicked ones escaping."

"Wicked ones like the pirate?"

"Men like the pirate."

"Don't let him escape, Sergeant... erm..."

"Private. Private Simpson."

"Pleased to meet you, Private Simpson. I'm Louisiana Le Moyne."

"Big name for a little lady."

"You can call me Lou. Everybody else does."

The man leaned forward. "I'm not sure I want to call you anything. I don't have to speak to a slave girl."

Lou smiled brightly. "Then I'll just go in," she told him.

"Then you just do that," said Private Simpson.

Lou entered the cool shade of the stone courthouse, through the heavy oak doors and into the courtroom itself. She was just in time to see the people rise lazily to their feet as the judge walked in.

"All rise for Judge Jenkins," a clerk cried a little late.

Lou slipped into a seat at the back and watched a grey-haired white man in black robes sit in the judge's chair. An Englishman, she decided.

Judge Jenkins shuffled some parchment in front of him. He looked across at the wooden box where a red-haired, wild-eyed man glared back.

"Are you Jack Greaves?"

About fifty people had crowded into the room to watch. They turned their eyes towards the prisoner. They waited for him to say, "I am."

Instead, he bellowed, "Who wants to know? Eh? What business is it of yours?"

CHAPTER TWO
SUGAR AND SCOT

Judge Jenkins blinked and his pale lips went tight with fury. "This may be the island of Nevis, but it is an English court of law. You will behave as if you are in England," he said quietly.

"I'm not English. I'm Scottish, just as my parents were Scottish, and I don't like you English."

The judge sighed. "If you're going to be foolish, I'll have you taken off to the cells and we'll have the trial without you."

"Pah," Greaves snorted and looked out through the high windows to the clear sky as if he didn't care.

"Are you the pirate known as Red-legs Greaves?" the judge asked.

"I'm a sugar farmer. I have twenty slaves and they're waiting for me back on my farm. If you lock me away, they won't know what to do. They'll starve."

"We will," Lou moaned softly.

"Before you were a sugar farmer, you were a pirate," the judge said slowly.

"Who says?" the Scotsman asked.

"I do," a man called out.

Lou turned and saw a large man in a fine blue suit with an expensive linen shirt.

The judge smiled. "Master Ellis!" he said in a voice as soft as a dove. "Step forward."

The rich man stood in front of the judge. "Ten years ago, I was sailing on one of my ships with a load of spice."

"And what happened, Master Ellis?"

Ellis turned, stretched out an arm and pointed at Greaves. "Red-legs Greaves there stopped my ship. He robbed me and left me penniless."

"Penniless?" Greaves roared. "Penniless? In a suit that cost more than a dozen slaves? You're a lying English toad, Ellis."

"Silence," the judge snapped. He turned to Master Ellis again and asked, "Tell me, why do you call him Dead-legs?"

"Red-legs, Your Honour. He's from Scotland. They wear kilts up there. Here in the Indies, their pale knees turn red. All the pirates called him Red-legs."

"And you saw his red legs when he robbed you?"

"I did, Your Honour."

The judge nodded. He pulled a square of black cloth from under his table. He placed it on his head. "Jack Red-legs Greaves, I sentence you to hang in chains. Tomorrow morning. May God have mercy on your soul."

"No!" Lou cried. "You can't do that to my master!"

CHAPTER THREE
SILENCE AND CELLS

"Silence in court," the judge said.

"But what will the slaves do without him?" Lou cried.

"The estate will belong to the court...
and we will sell it. You will have a new
master," the judge said.

"I'll buy it," Master Ellis said.

"Good man," the judge said, smiling.
"It's probably worth a thousand pounds."

"I'll give you five hundred... cash," Ellis
said.

Judge Jenkins nodded. "You can pay
me later."

"But Master Greaves is a wonderful master," Lou argued. "He's the kindest slave owner on the whole of Nevis Island. Everybody says so."

"Silence in court."

"Master Ellis is a monster – he beats and whips and starves his slaves," the girl went on.

"Only the lazy ones," Ellis sneered. "And the cheeky ones. There is a whip in my house just waiting for you when I take over."

"Master Greaves is right – you're a toad. A fat, slimy toad," Lou wailed.

"Silence in court, girl, or I'll whip you myself," the judge shouted.

"It isn't fair," Lou sobbed.

"That's enough. Your master will spend the night in the dungeon below the courthouse. He will hang in chains at sunrise. And *you*, girl, will spend the night with him. That will teach you to hold your evil little tongue. Private... take them both down to the cells."

Red-legs Greaves shook his head. "Oh, Lou, you foolish child. What have you done?"

"Spoken up for you, Master Greaves," she said, as she was pushed down the gloomy stairs toward the prison cell. "I thought the English were famous for being fair. Well, they're not. You haven't been a pirate for years."

They entered the filthy cell and the door closed behind them with a boom like the sound of doom. Red-legs Greaves walked to the small window and looked out through the bars. "I've had a lucky life. When it ends tomorrow, I won't complain."

Lou didn't answer.

The tears she sniffed back were making her throat too tight to speak.

CHAPTER FOUR
CROMWELL AND KILLING

Red-legs Greaves scraped green scum off
the water bucket in the
corner and scooped
it over his ruddy
face. "I'm sorry to
leave you like this,"
he sighed.

"You've been such
a good master," Lou
whimpered.

The Scot nodded. "Aye. That's because
I know what it's like to be a slave. I was
born into slavery."

Lou looked up, wide-eyed. "You? A slave? But you're a white man."

He shrugged. "Back in Britain there was a man called Oliver Cromwell. He cut off the head of King Charles and then he captured all the king's friends. My mother and father fought for the king. When they lost, Cromwell sold them as slaves and had them sent to Barbados. That's where I was born. A slave."

"But how did you become a pirate?" the girl asked.

"My parents died... the heat and the diseases did for them. I was sold to a master who enjoyed beating me. So one night I decided to escape. There was just one way off the island – "

"A boat?"

Red-legs laughed. "Aye. I swam across Carlisle Bay to the main harbour in Bridgetown. About two miles. Then I hid on board a ship so I could sail away and make my fortune."

"And did you?"

"Lord, no, lassie. How was I to know it was a pirate ship I was hiding on? The captain was the wicked Captain Hawkins."

"Wicked?"

"Aye. He wasn't happy robbing traders. He had to torture the captured crews for fun and then he killed them – even the women. When he found me, he said I had to work for him, or die."

"So you became a pirate for Captain Hawkins," Lou said. "But if you killed all the people you robbed... how is Master Ellis still alive? If you'd killed him, he wouldn't be there in court."

Red-legs Greaves held up his hands. "No, young Lou. I said Captain Hawkins was a ruthless, killing pirate. But *I* only ever killed one man. And that was the best day's work I ever did."

Lou's mouth fell open. "Oh, Master Greaves, who did you kill?"

"Ah, young Lou, that comes later in my story. You'll have to wait and see..."

CHAPTER FIVE
BARS AND BREAD

As the sun sank lower in the sky, it grew a little cooler in the cell. Red-legs Greaves stood at the bars of the cell and looked out. Lou was too short to see over the windowsill.

The iron bars were as rusty and red as Master Greaves's legs. The man tugged at them. They rattled, but all his strength couldn't pull them out.

A guard brought them a bottle of wine, some fresh water and a plate of bread and ham. "Wine? Ham? A fine meal for a poor prisoner!" the Scot cried.

The guard shuffled his feet and looked at the floor. "We always give a good meal to the men we're going to hang."

"Ah! You send them to Hell with a full belly?" Red-legs said, and laughed.

Lou groaned. "You aren't going to Hell, Master Greaves. You were the kindest master on the island. Everybody said that."

"But I killed a man, remember."

"Who was it?"

The Scot poured a little wine into the cup and added water. He gave it to Lou. "I spent a year on Hawkins's ship," he said. "I soon found that all the crew hated him. They hated his cruel ways. He was even cruel to his own men. If anyone crossed him, he had them marooned."

"What's that?"

"A marooned man is set down on a desert island with a little food and a pistol. If he's lucky, he may shoot something, like a goat, and eat a little. But when the powder and the bullets run out, he'll slowly starve to death. It's something all pirates are afraid of."

Lou shook her head. "But if you hated him so much, why didn't you all get together and maroon *him*?" Lou asked.

"Two reasons. Captain Hawkins was a powerful man and no one had the courage to fight him. And he was a *good* pirate. He led us to many rich ships, stole a lot of treasure and made us all a fortune."

"Like Master Ellis," Lou said sadly. "The cruel and the wicked get rich."

Red-legs nodded slowly as he chewed on a piece of ham. "But, like me, even the rich can't buy their life. Not when it's time to die."

"Captain Hawkins died?"

"He did."

"How? Tell me!" Lou cried.

The Scot tasted the ham as if it were the last meal he'd ever eat. He smacked his lips, sipped a little wine and ran a hand over his mouth. "Captain Hawkins met a man who was foolish enough to fight him."

"Who?" Lou asked softly.

"Me," Red-legs Greaves replied.

CHAPTER SIX
SWORDS AND SUNSET

"We saw a French spice ship just off the island of Saint Kitts," Red-legs Greaves explained. "She was a fast ship and it took us all day to catch her. That upset Captain Hawkins. By the time we came alongside the Frenchie, his blood was boiling with rage. He gave us the order to kill everyone."

"You couldn't do that," Lou said.

"They were simple sailors, with no guns and no swords. Just the knives they used to eat their food. 'I'm not doing it,' I told Hawkins. 'There's no need to kill the crew. Let's just take their spice and sell it in Bridgetown. No one has to get hurt!'"

"Was he angry?" Lou asked.

"I think Captain Hawkins was too *shocked* to be angry. No one ever argued with him. He just stared at me. Then he said, 'How many sailors are there on that French ship, Greaves?' I looked across the sea and said, 'Twenty.' And he drew his cutlass and said, 'There are twenty-one men going to die today. You are number one.' Then he rushed at me with his sword raised in the air."

"But you drew your sword?" Lou asked.

"I never carried a sword. I was a sailor – I mended the sails and steered the ship, I scrubbed the decks and loaded supplies. I wasn't a fighter."

"But you beat Captain Hawkins?"

"He rushed at me. His arm was raised high in the air. He thought I would run away. Instead, I ran towards him. I grabbed his sword arm. And twisted it. He was a strong man, but his fine leather boots skidded on the deck and he fell... on his sword. I still hear his cry in my nightmares. He dropped to his knees. His eyes grew cloudy. He tried to pluck the sword from his side, but his hands were shaking too much."

"And he died," Lou said.

Red-legs shook his head. "The next thing I remember, the crew were cheering.

They threw Hawkins's body over the side and raised me up on their shoulders. Then they told me I was their new captain."

"So that's how you became a pirate," Lou said. "I bet you were a *good* pirate."

The sun had now set and clouds over Nevis Peak blotted out the stars. In the perfect darkness, Red-legs said, "A pirate is a pirate. And a captured pirate is a dead pirate. Wake me when the sky grows light. I want to see my last sunrise."

Minutes later, the old pirate was snoring softly while the young slave girl quietly prayed.

"Hello, God. God? Are you there? Master Greaves used to be a pirate. But he's a good, kind man. Do you think you could do one of your miracles to get him free? Thank you, God."

CHAPTER SEVEN
SUNRISE AND SCREAMS

Lou woke to see the clouds were a pearly grey colour. It was only an hour till sunrise. She shook the pirate gently. "Master Greaves. You wanted me to wake you before dawn."

The old man shook his head and splashed water over his face. "Thanks, lassie." He sat up and looked at her. "I wish there was something I could do for you. I know Master Ellis will treat you badly. That will be his revenge."

"Because you robbed him?"

"Aye. When I became a pirate captain, I set down new rules. We could jump on board a trading ship. We could push the crew aside – even tie them up – and steal their cargo. But none of my men must shed a drop of blood. The crew liked the new rules as much as they'd hated old Captain Hawkins."

"What did you do if they *did* hurt somebody?"

"We'd pay the man his share of the treasure we'd won... and put him ashore at the nearest port."

Lou's eyes shone with pride. "So you were a *kind* pirate?"

"I tried not to hurt anyone. Mind you, the victims still didn't like it. I remember robbing James Ellis' ship. When we went on board, he started firing pistols at the crew. He hit one lad in the leg, so we had to rush at him when he tried to reload. Then we tied him to the mast. The lad that was hit was upset. He went and pulled Ellis' pants down... and the ladies on the ship all laughed."

"That would make him angry," Lou said wisely.

"He was ranting about what he'd do to us. He said he'd see us all hang from the gallows... and now he's going to get his wish."

"But you gave up pirating years ago."

"We did well. We made a fortune... even the lowly deck scrubbers went home rich. I had enough money to buy a sugar farm here on Nevis Island and enough left over to buy a dozen slaves. That was fifteen years ago, before you were born. Yesterday, I went to the market, and Ellis spotted me. You know the rest."

Lou's eyes filled with tears. "I prayed for a miracle," she murmured.

The Scot ruffled her hair and laughed. "You're a good child. Maybe the rope will snap and I'll end up with a broken leg instead of a broken neck. Maybe that will be your miracle."

"How can you joke about it?" she gasped.

Somewhere above them, they heard a heavy door open. Footsteps clumped down the stairs. Keys rattled on the jailer's fist.

Lou backed up against the wall. The bucket of slimy water stood by her side. The smooth surface began to ripple. The bucket trembled. The timbers in the cell creaked.

There was a huge crash as stones fell from the roof and the walls of the courthouse crumbled. Through the bars of the window came a roar and the clear morning air was filled with the dust of a hundred tumbling buildings. Screams of the people mixed with the roar of falling stone.

Lou felt the solid cell wall at her back shaking. "What's happening?" she squeaked in terror.

Red-legs Greaves gave a thin smile. "Earthquake," he said.

Chapter Eight
Dust and Destruction

Lou huddled in a corner as the courthouse began to fall. Their cell below the ground cracked and dust filled the air until it was as dark as night again. There were more great shudders like the trembling body of a dying giant. Then, slowly, all fell silent.

Stones trickled through the twisted bars of the cell. Lou spat the thick dust from her mouth and coughed. "Master Greaves?"

"I'm here, child."

"Are you hurt?"

The man chuckled. "Takes more than a little earthquake to kill a Scot. In fact, they'll all be a bit too busy to hang me this morning. I've seen it before on these islands. It's the rich folk in their stone houses that suffer most."

Lou nodded. The dust was settling and she could see her master, red hair turned white with stone dust and ruddy face ghost-pale. "The slaves in the tar-paper shacks should be safe enough. Should I go and see?"

"There's a whole courthouse fallen on top of those stairs, lassie. You'll never get out that way," the man said gently.

"No," Lou told him. "But the bars have come away from the window. Look. I can squeeze through."

Red-legs Greaves walked across the cracked cell floor, ducking under the broken beams. He tugged at the row of bars and they fell with a clatter into the room. The dusty air outside was still. The way was open.

"Looks like your prayer was answered, lassie," the man said. "You go first and give a hand to pull me out."

A minute later, the two prisoners stood in the shattered street and looked around. People, bleeding and bruised, dazed and dying, lay amongst the ruins of the town. "Shall we help them?" Lou asked.

The man shook his head slowly. "The earthquake shakes the sea, too. In an hour or so, some huge waves could wash over the island. If we patch them up, we'll be saving them for the sea to drown."

"Will we drown, too?" the girl groaned.

"There are just two safe places – on top of Nevis Peak, or out at sea."

"Have we time to climb the mountain?" Lou asked.

"No, but we do have time to run to the harbour and take a ship. Come on, lassie, run! Run for your life!"

CHAPTER NINE
LUCK AND LOUISIANA

They ran. They ran through the torn town and down to the harbour where dazed sailors were wandering in wonder at the sight all around them.

"What about my friends, the other slaves?" Lou moaned.

"The estate is high enough up," Master Greaves panted as he hurried behind the girl. "They'll be safe. There'll be so few people left on the island, they'll be able to find their own freedom."

"Freedom," Lou repeated, and ran on.

The captain of a sugar ship stood on deck, as still and stiff as the main mast on his ship.

"Captain McKay!" Red-legs Greaves shouted. "Are you sailing with my sugar crop today?"

"I... I was going to... but... but..." the man burbled.

"Then cast off at once," the old pirate ordered.

"Yes, Master Greaves, but I don't have a full crew. Just two men stayed on board. We don't know where the rest are."

Red-legs grinned. "You have an old sea dog and a runaway slave to help. Now cast off before the great wave hits the island and wets my good sugar."

The captain stirred into life and shouted at his two sailors to make ready to leave. "Where to, Master Greaves?" one asked.

The old pirate wrapped an arm around the thin shoulders of the girl in the tattered dress. "Where to, Lou?"

"To freedom, Master Greaves... to freedom!"

When they reached the safety of another shore, their adventure was over. The sugar was sold and Red-legs Greaves used the money to buy a small sugar plantation on a distant island where no one knew him.

The plantation was popular with all the workers because Red-legs Greaves was such a good master. His manager was a young lady who called herself Miss Louisiana Le Moyne... though Greaves always called her simply Lou.

The years passed, and master and manager shared a table on the porch of the fine house he had built for them.

"You could be the richest man on the island, if you wanted," Lou told him as they looked out across the bay to the sea as green as emeralds. "And if you didn't give away so much to the poor."

"When you are as lucky as me, you need to share your luck around. I was a pirate once, and now I'm paying back my treasure to the people who need it the most."

Lou smiled. She knew he was right. "Though there are some things money can't buy, old master."

"Are there, young Lou? And what in the world might they be?"

"Miracles, master. Miracles."

And the old Scotsman didn't argue.

Epilogue

In the story, Lou is made up – but the rest of the tale is true.

Red-legs Greaves was a Scotsman, born into slavery, who escaped to become a pirate with the ruthless Captain Hawkins. He was forced to kill Hawkins when they fell out.

He took over the pirate ship but he refused to kill or torture, and made sure his pirates harmed none of the men they fought. Red-legs made a fortune with his raids and retired to start a sugar plantation on Nevis Island. But an angry victim of his piracy betrayed him and he was arrested.

The judge said the Scotsman should hang, but the day before the execution an earthquake destroyed his prison. Many guards and prisoners were killed, but Red-legs managed to escape and enjoy his freedom again. It was a miracle.

He joined the crew of a whaling ship and served the captain well. He became a pirate-hunter and helped to capture a gang of pirates that had been ruining the whaling fleet.

The king of England gave Red-legs a pardon for his good work. The old pirate settled onto a new plantation, where he was loved for his kindness. He died peacefully of old age ... unlike most pirates of the time.

You try

1. A plea for freedom

Imagine YOU are Red-legs, caught and taken to court. The judge looks grim – you think he is going to send you off to be hanged. But before he passes sentence he says you can plead for your life.

Tell him why you should NOT hang for your crimes. The judge wants his dinner, so you can't go on too long! You can have only a hundred words to make your plea, not one word more.

You may begin, "Your Honour, I admit I'm guilty of those crimes, but..."

You have just 90 more words to save your life!

2. Kilted criminal

Red-legs must have looked quite odd. Some pirates made themselves look fierce to scare their enemies.

One famous pirate, Blackbeard, was a tall, thin man with a very black beard which he wore very long. His thick, black beard was knotted into pigtails, sometimes tied with small, coloured ribbons. He wore knee-length boots and dark clothing, topped with a wide hat and sometimes a long coat of brightly coloured silk or velvet. In battle, Blackbeard wore a belt over his shoulders, with six pistols fastened there. He even stuck lighted rope under his hat so he looked like a terrifying monster.

Can you draw a fierce pirate... but wearing a kilt, like Red-legs?